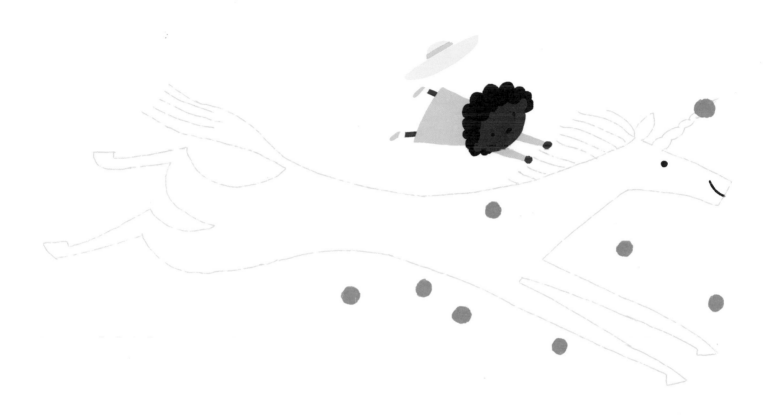

This unicorn belongs to:

....

For Naomi and Olla – G. D.

For Maiya – A. B.

First published in the United Kingdom in 2020 by
Thames & Hudson Ltd, 181A High Holborn, London WC1V 7QX

If I had a unicorn © 2020 Thames & Hudson Ltd, London
Text © 2020 Gabby Dawnay
Illustrations © 2020 Alex Barrow

British Library Cataloguing-in-Publication Data
A catalogue record for this book is available from the British Library

ISBN 978-0-500-65226-8

Printed and bound in China by Everbest Printing Co. Ltd

To find out about all our publications, please visit
www.thamesandhudson.com. There you can
subscribe to our e-newsletter, browse or download
our current catalogue, and buy any titles that are in print.

GABBY DAWNAY
ALEX BARROW

If I had a unicorn

I think I'd like a

We've got
a garden

A   would be awesome

but there's no spare
room at home...

I couldn't keep a

(we don't live by the sea)...

A   would be kind of cool

but way too hot for me!

I really want a rainbow pet,
a little like a horse
with lots of extra superpowers...
a unicorn, of course!

Oh if I had a **UNICORN**
each day I'd make a wish.
My unicorn would toss his mane
and grant it with a 'swish'!

For breakfast we'd eat jelly.
For lunch we'd nibble cakes.

For tea we'd munch on cookies,
dipped in dreamy chocolate shakes!

My unicorn would click his hooves –
we'd travel far and wide...

BEEP!

Each day a new adventure.
Just imagine – what a ride!

Unicorns are magic,
I'm pretty sure they fly.
They like to take their exercise
across a rainbow sky!

If I had a unicorn we'd make the garden grow...

...with every single blossom in a flower-power show!

Unicorns spread glitter –
they like to keep things sweet.

My unicorn would run around
and make stuff nice and neat!

With unicorns you don't get sad,
nor grumpy, mad or cross.
Because each time you start to frown
they give you candyfloss!

Their favourite food is ice-cream.
I wonder if they do
a multicoloured, fluffy sort of

unicorny...

...!

If I had a unicorn
the games that we would play...
I'd wash and style his silky tail
and plait his mane each day!

Unicorns are very rare.
They're loyal, kind and true.
Perhaps if you wish hard enough
there might be one for YOU!

If you'd rather have a giant pet,
you might like to read
If I had a dinosaur.

Or for a more relaxing story,
why not try
If I had a sleepy sloth?